Broc and Cara's Picnic Party

written by Dave A. Wilson

illustrated by Melissa Bailey

Thanks to Joan Patrick and Rob Wilson,
my mentors who have been with me every step of the way.

Thanks Mom and Dad! You always encouraged creativity
and the pursuit of dreams with all of your children.

Thanks for the musical support of Canadian Juno winner
Charlie Hope!

For Sam.
Your birth woke Daddy up.

I work in this garden
the whole day through.
I'm Buzzy the Bee,
so nice to meet you!

I'm cute and I'm furry and never unkind,
with a big yellow face and a bumble BEE -hind!

I swoop and I dip to my flower destination.

Many plants depend on my **BEE** pollination!

Zip Zip over here.

Zoom Zoom right on through.

When you care for this garden, it will take care of

YOU!

From the orchard and garden

take a bite of real food.

Juice a rainbow of colour

for a sunshiny mood!

You are what you eat.

We'll mix, match, and blend.
Let's all drink some more!

This tasty adventure is

FUN

for your tummy!

Here's my good buddy Broc
to explain it to you!

Yo yo Broc here,

and some say I'm mighty.

The reason's up here.

I've got Super Dudes inside me!

SUPER DUDES

are vitamins,

phytonutrients, too.

Take a bite,

chew and swallow,

and we'll energize you!

You'll grow and be **HEALTHY**,

and filled with nutrition.

Eat the Dudes Every Day!

Why did Dave A. Wilson write this book? He wanted a fun way to encourage big kids like him and little kids like his son Sam to eat their veggies.

Dave lives in Victoria, British Columbia.

This is his first book.

Check us out at

BROCandCARA.COM

for FREE t-shirt designs, mini posters,
puppets, games and more!

Made in the USA
Lexington, KY
19 March 2018